What is the biggest ant in the world?

For Jemima, happy finding-out time! x x ~ T. C.

For Isaac x ~ T. W.

tiger tales
5 River Road, Suite 128, Wilton, CT 06897
Published in the United States 2014
Originally published in Great Britain 2014
by Little Tiger Press
Text copyright © 2014 Tracey Corderoy
Illustrations copyright © 2014 Tim Warnes
Visit Tim Warnes at www.ChapmanandWarnes.com
ISBN-13: 978-1-58925-168-7
ISBN-10: 1-58925-168-7
Printed in China
LTP/1400/0888/0314
All rights reserved
10 9 8 7 6 5 4 3 2 1

For more insight and activities,
visit us at www.tigertalesbooks.com

Why?

by Tracey Corderoy

Illustrated by Tim Warnes

tiger tales

Otto was a rhino with a
LOT of questions.

Sometimes, when he was finding the answers,
Otto made a little bit of a mess . . . .

Why does toast make crumbs?

Why is milk splashy?

And sometimes Otto made a LOT of messes!

Why do dropped things go SMASH?

Otto! Why don't you go and find Daddy?

But wherever Otto went . . .

. . . his questions went, too.

Why is mud so sticky, Daddy?

Why are these roots so long?

Otto's parents decided that a rhino with a LOT of questions might like a trip to the museum.

The museum was amazing.
There was SO much to see!

←Antiquities

Some of these questions were **easy** to answer...

PRESS HERE to hear me ROAR!

Tricera

Mommy, **Why** aren't there any dinosaurs NOW?

...but others were a **little** more tricky.

Daddy, **Why** does that man have such big ears?

Why is her nose so long?

Otto loved the museum. There were buttons and knobs and things that bleeped, buzzed, and clanged!

Off he went—
here, there, and
everywhere....

MANY whys later, there was
still SO much to find out.

"Daddy," said Otto,
now quite sleepy,
"why do...
robots...
go..."

YAWN!

Suddenly, all of Otto's questions stopped.

Otto was quiet **all** the way home.

And he didn't say a
word during his snack ...   OR at bath time.

As they turned out his light, Mommy and Daddy wondered if Otto had run out of questions.

But why would they **EVER** think that?